THIS BOOK
BELONGS TO:

Beauty
and the Beast

From a fairy story by CHARLES PERRAULT
retold by ROBERT MATHIAS

Illustrated by ANNABEL SPENCELEY

Derrydale Books

NEW YORK

A TEMPLAR BOOK

This 1991 edition published by Derrydale Books,
distributed by Outlet Book Company, Inc., a Random House Company,
225 Park Avenue South, New York, New York 10003.

Devised and produced by The Templar Company plc,
Pippbrook Mill, London Road, Dorking, Surrey RH4 1JE, Great Britain.

Edited by A J Wood
Designed by Mike Jolley
Printed and bound in Malaysia

ISBN 0-517-06693-9
87654321

FOREWORD

Beauty and the Beast is probably the most famous and enduring of Charles Perrault's fairy stories. Variations of the story have been told throughout Europe for generations. The story's magical atmosphere and the contrasting characters of the beautiful maiden and the grotesque beast who fall in love, provide more than a simple romance. Like so many well-loved fables it also carries a valued moral. It has been a favorite with children since the day it was first written.

Long ago there lived a wealthy merchant. He was very rich, but his greatest treasures were his three beautiful daughters. Although he loved them all, it was the youngest, a girl of tender kindness and fragile beauty, who was his favorite. One day the merchant made ready to sail away on a voyage of trade. He sent for his daughters to ask what gifts they would like from the lands across the sea.

"Oh, Sir," trilled the first, "a hand-glass, made of silver and gold, so I may admire my beauty."

"And for me a crown," cooed the second. "Sparkling with jewels and suited to my rank."

The merchant sighed and turned to the youngest daughter. "And you, my child, what is your desire?"

"A rose, dear father, to please my heart. Just a perfect rose of the darkest red."

The merchant sailed away in a fine ship and for many months he traded with men from far-off lands. Some bowed and scraped and, smiling sideways, eyed his purse to clip his price. Some stood, stony-faced to drive a harder bargain, then laughed and clapped their hands on his to seal the bond. The merchant bartered carpets for canvas and silks for spices, wine for wood and cotton for carvings – and all the while his wealth increased.

His business done, he sought to buy the promised gifts. He found a hand-glass, all silver and gold, and a well-bred crown, sparkling bright, but a perfect rose of darkest red? Where should he look? In the gardens of kings and the lands of lords he saw many fine blooms, but none was perfect. Was there not a finer rose elsewhere perhaps?

With troubled thoughts, the merchant sailed for home. Somewhere he had still to find the perfect rose to please his youngest daughter's heart. He could not bear to return home without a gift for her, his precious, fragile beauty.

At night he paced the ship's deck, unable to sleep. As the sun rose, he watched the dolphins playing in the ship's wake and the fire-crested waves breaking beneath the bows.

One morning at dawn he rubbed his tired eyes and stared out at the empty sea. As he watched, a pirate ship appeared as if from nowhere. The merchant sprang to turn his ship around and make for safety, but it was not to be.

The wind was in the brigand's favor and in no time they were close by. To the merchant's horror, they leapt aboard with snarling faces and took his boat and all his gold and goods. They laughed and cast him overboard into the rolling sea. He swam for his life until, exhausted, he was washed up on the shore of a strange island.

The merchant stood alone on the beach and looked towards the sea. There was no sign of his ship or his crew. He turned and stumbled into the gloom of the forest behind him. At first he tripped and tumbled over vines and roots, unable to find his way, but as his eyes grew accustomed to the dappled sunshine filtering through the trees, his progress became easier.

He looked down and saw that he was walking along a pathway flagged with broad stones. He followed the path through the trees and became aware of a strange silence. No birds sang from the tree tops, no creature scurried in the undergrowth, and no breeze rustled the leaves.

Suddenly, as he came upon a clearing, he saw a magnificent palace standing on a green hill. It gleamed in the morning light as if it was cut from the purest crystal.

As the merchant approached the palace, the eerie silence of the forest gave way to the faint sound of sweet music. He could see that the palace windows and the great arched gateway were thrown wide open.

There was no one to be seen so he walked through the gate into a beautiful garden. It was filled with exotic flowers of every shape and color. Trees laden with fruit dipped down, kissing their reflections in crystal-clear pools that darted with golden fishes.

Inside the palace elegant furniture stood in the hallways, fine carpets littered the polished floors, the walls were hung with silk brocades, and all the fittings gleamed with gold. A palace fit for a king, he thought, but the place was empty of life – it was deserted.

Tired after his trek through the forest, the merchant slumped into a chair. He felt hungry and wondered if such a grand palace possessed a kitchen and some food. But the thought had hardly crossed his mind when a table appeared before him. It was laden with food and wine fit for a banquet. There were bowls of plump and juicy fruit, sides of beef and ham, nuts and crusty bread, and flagons of spring water and ruby wine.

The merchant ate his fill and, tipping back the last tankard of wine, he yawned. He was almost asleep on his feet as he climbed the staircase to the upper chambers.

Finding a bedchamber to his liking, he kicked off his boots and stretched out on the great, soft bed. In no time at all he was fast asleep and snoring loudly.

Early the next morning he was woken by the bright shafts of sunlight dancing through the tall, narrow windows. He pulled on his boots and stared out over the gardens. His eyes opened wide in delight and a smile creased his face. There, in a small grassy clearing, was a rose bush and on it bloomed a dark red rose. He rushed outside into the sunshine to see it more clearly.

To the merchant's delight, the rose was perfect – its perfume exquisite, its bloom magical, and its color the darkest of reds. With a happy heart, he reached out and plucked it from the bush. At last he had found the rose to please his daughter's heart.

But as soon as he picked the beautiful flower, the sky blackened, lightning flashed, and a crack of thunder split the angry sky. Then, from behind him, came a terrifying roar that shook the earth beneath his feet.

The merchant spun round in terror. Towering over him, he saw a grotesquely misshapen creature. A terrible being, neither man nor animal – a raging, ugly Beast!

"So, this is the thanks you show for my kindness!" said the Beast in a voice that was a low, hideous growl. "I gave you good food and let you use my home as if it were your own, yet you choose to steal the rose I cherish."

The merchant trembled with fear.

"So, now you shall die!" the Beast continued.

"But the rose was not for me," stammered the terrified merchant. "It was for my child, the sweetest of my daughters."

The Beast drew back, his twisted brows clenched in thought.

"So be it. Let your child take your place here. Let her come of her own free will and I will let you live." So saying, the Beast reached into a pocket and, extending his huge paw, dropped a golden ring into the merchant's hand.

"Take this ring and guard it carefully. Within three days, she must be here or you will die!"

The merchant stared down at the ring in dismay. How could he let his lovely daughter take his place here, with this terrible creature? But when he looked up the Beast had vanished and, to his amazement, he found himself in his own home, the rose and the ring still clasped in his hands.

When the merchant told his story, his youngest daughter threw her arms around his neck.

"Dear father, I will gladly take your place," she said. My love is strong and the Beast will surely let me return to you soon."

"My child, I pray it will be so," said the merchant sadly.

A little cross at not receiving their promised gifts, his elder daughters questioned him more. Surely the Beast could not really harm them. Why should they not just keep the golden ring? But the merchant remained silent and said nothing for three days.

On the third day he watched with a heavy heart as his favorite daughter took up the rose and slipped the ring on her finger. In a flash she found herself standing by the rose bush in the enchanted garden. The rose lifted from her hand and bound itself to the severed stem where it bloomed brighter than before.

The music that played through the trees and the scent of the flowers filled her with delight. Soon she came upon the beautiful palace and, walking through the great doorway, she marvelled at the many fine rooms and felt at ease, unafraid. When dusk fell she went into the great hall to dine. As she expected, the table was set with dishes of delicate flavor and taste, served in the finest crystal and porcelain.

As she began to eat, to her amazement the marble wall in front of her began to glow like the embers of a winter fire. She peered closer and saw letters appear from the tiny flames, sparkling together to form these words:

Welcome, pure Beauty, and have no fear
For you are truly Mistress here.

No sooner had she read the message, than the flames disappeared. Beauty looked around her but to her disappointment there was no one in sight. The great palace was silent still, save for the sound of gentle music.

Each day the merchant's youngest daughter awoke to a new delight: the finest silk gowns were laid out for her choice; the sweetest food was always to her taste; and the gardens sang with soft music. The sweet-scented blooms parted before her, allowing her to pass unheeded. And when she was tired, her feet were lifted and she was carried along as if on a summer's breeze.

Day followed day and she grew fond of her unseen master. It was clear that he loved her dearly. Each evening she read the fiery words that appeared, full of sweet messages, on the marble wall, but she longed to hear his voice and begged him to speak to her directly. At last he relented and wrote these final words of fire:

So, let it then be soon.
Go to the garden at noon.
There, Beauty, say: "Speak to me."

The following day she went to the garden well before noon. She was so excited at the thought of hearing her master's voice that she laughed and skipped among the flowers. At last the sun was high overhead and the shadow on the sun-dial darkened the mid-day mark. Quietly she said:

"Speak to me."

For a moment there was silence, then, from behind a thicket, she heard a long sigh. Again there was a pause, broken by a terrible snarling voice that roared through the silence, tearing at her senses and filling her with terror. She clutched at her breast yet

stood her ground. Despite her fear she listened. At length she heard just words of love and kindness, and no longer noticed the fearsome voice which spoke them. Her fear vanished and from that moment the Beast and the Beauty spoke each day.

As time passed Beauty longed, not just to hear her master's voice, but to see him as well. Again she pleaded with him, urging him to show himself.

"No, dear Beauty, I cannot," he said in answer. "I am afraid that should you see my beastly form, I will in turn see only loathing in your eyes."

She began to cry and her tears softened his heart so much that he agreed to her wish.

"Come to the garden at dusk, when the shadows are at their deepest. Then say 'Show yourself, dear friend,' and I will do so."

At dusk she said the chosen words. A movement close at hand caused her to turn. For a fleeting second the Beast was revealed, and in that instant she saw a creature so terrible that she cried out in alarm and fell senseless to the ground.

When at last she opened her eyes she saw the huge form of the Beast nearby. He sat among the beautiful flowers of his garden with his back toward her. To her dismay, she saw that his shoulders shook with dreadful sobs as he wept bitterly. Suddenly she no longer felt afraid. She walked toward him and rested her hand on his arm.

The Beast raised his tear-stained face and turned his sad eyes up toward her. Her kind heart was filled with sorrow, for Beauty knew that it was she who had caused him such pain.

"Do not cry," she whispered. "I do not fear your form. It is only the shell that cloaks a tender heart. The wisdom that lies within is good and true. Please forgive me for hurting you so."

So saying, she took her lace handkerchief and gently wiped a tear from his cheek. At her touch, the terrible face creased in a smile. From that day, they became loving friends and thereafter delighted in each other's company, sharing in all the beauty of the strange island – the oak-like Beast and the delicate, fragile Beauty.

One night the merchant's daughter slept
fitfully. She tossed and turned on her bed and woke
with a start from a terrible dream. She cried out and
the Beast rushed to her side. Her dream had been of
her dear father, sick in his bed and close to death. The
Beast tried to comfort her, but his kind heart knew
that she would not rest until she stood by her father's
side. He bade her go and return to her home.

"Go now, Beauty," he said kindly, "but remember, you must return within three days. Should you fail to return within that time then I will die. My love for you is such that I cannot live without you."

Beauty smiled up at him and nodded tenderly. She took the golden ring he offered and slipped it on her finger.

Her father was so pleased to see his beloved daughter that within a couple of days he was dancing about in the best of health. She told her story and of her love for the Beast. Her eldest sister snorted and the second sister scowled:

"If he is so ugly, does he not deserve to die?"

"Dear sister," replied Beauty. "That is an unworthy thought. I could not be so cruel to so kind and gentle a being."

Her sisters turned away consumed with envy of her happiness. But their spite got the better of them and, as the last hour of the third day ticked away, they turned back the hands of the clock. The youngest sister waited, impatient to return to the Beast. At last she could wait no more and, saying goodbye, slipped the ring on her finger and vanished – back to the enchanted palace.

The palace was silent, no birds sang in the gardens and no music played through the chambers. She searched for the Beast and at last, in the clearing where the rose bush grew, she found him. He lay still on the ground and clutched to his breast was the single, dark red rose. It fluttered in the gentle breeze and she knew at once that he was dead.

She knelt beside him and rested her hand on his twisted brow. She felt the tears well in her eyes and bent slowly to kiss his cheek. A single tear fell onto the Beast's heart as her eyes filled with the pain of sorrow and the daylight clouded from sunlight to dusk. Falling, she gave up her senses and slumped over the dead body of the Beast.

Her eyes opened in surprise to the chatter of a hundred voices. She was sitting on a silver throne and standing beside her was a handsome prince. He smiled kindly down at her. The hall before her was full of noblemen and their ladies. Among them she saw her father, his hands clasped together, beaming broadly. Her two sisters, smiling sheepishly, stood beside him.

Beauty was about to start down the steps toward them when the prince took her hand and spoke softly. There was something familiar about the way he picked his words.

"Dear Beauty," he began, "as a child I was cursed by an evil witch. She cast a spell on me and turned me into a grotesque beast banished from my kingdom, a monster too terrible for people to behold. But for your love I would have remained so, despised and feared for the rest of my life. You saw beneath the ugliness and broke the spell. I have come to love you truly and would now ask that you be my queen, and stay with me...forever."

And so she did.

The End